HERMELIN

the Detective Mouse

D0247418

700041841682

Red Fox

Well, I was trying out the new binoculars that I'd found in my breakfast cereal that morning.

I'd better introduce myself.

I am Hermelin.

The first thing I can
remember is waking up
in my cheese box (which smelled
delicious) and finding
I could read the name on it.

It said:

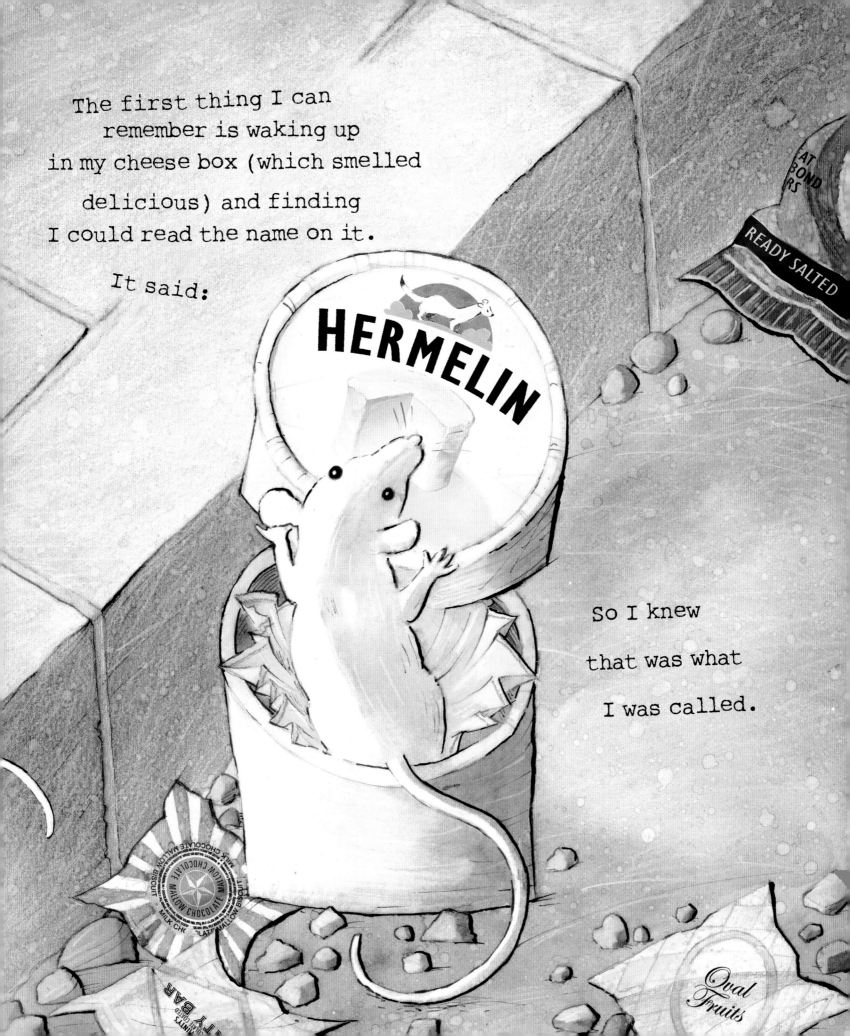

HERMELIN

So I knew
that was what
I was called.

Then I found this attic.
It is at the top of
Number 33 Offley Street.

It is full of
books and boxes
and boots,
and also
a typewriter.

Well, it was just after lunchtime in Offley Street, and I was passing the OFFLEY STREET NOTICE BOARD, and I had a good look at it.

OFFLEY STREET

LOST BAG
It belongs to Mrs Mattison. Black leather containing life savings.
Tel: 0207 946 0265

GONE! Have you seen my Teddy BoBo? He is maybe Lost. TeLL Imogen SPLotts.

Desperately Seeking PARSLEY
Greenish fur. Distinguished meow. Partial to fish. Greatly missed. Reports to Captain Potts, 31 Offley St.

Missing!
My reading glasses have disappeared. If found, notify Dr Parker at No. 25

DISAPPEARED!
MY BELOVED GOLDFISH
LUCKY
IS GONE FROM HIS BOWL
Any sightings, contact Bernardo Bosher at
BOSHER'S SAUSAGE SHOP
37 OFFLEY STREET

TELECOM

MAN
WITH
VAN
all Andy
07700 900843

VANISHED!
My priceless Diamond Bracelet
is **LOST** (perhaps stolen)

GENEROUS REWARD
No Questions Asked
Contact Lady Chumley-Plumley

Have you seen
my notebook?
I would really like it back —
contains vital information.
Emily
at No. 33
P.S. To whoever is
eating my cornflakes —
Help yourself!

I thought to myself:

Great
Heavens!

Just LOOK
at all these
lost things!

THESE

POOR PEOPLE

OF

OFFLEY STREET

NEED

SOME

HELP!

And I knew
I was just the one
for the job.

So I got to work.

Mrs Mattison's handbag was easy to locate.

I taped a note to her teapot.

GARBAGE GOBBLER

There's no time to type but maybe I can use the notebook.

Dear McMumbo, Please hurry. Baby McMumbo is in bin and in peril! Hermelin

I struggle with the stubby pencil; my paws are not good at this sort of thing.

FOLD

FOLD

When the message is written I fold it as quick as I can . . .

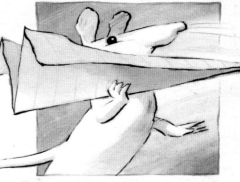

. . . into an aeroplane shape that will fly well,

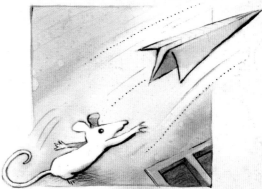

and with the last of my strength I hurl the plane towards Mr McMumbo's open window . . .

On Friday I saw there was a Report in Emily's *Offley Times*.

Mr McMumbo just managed to reach the Munch-u-lator Automatic Garbage Gobbler in time.

The next morning on the notice board there was a message for ME!

INVITATION

Dear Hermelin,

We don't know who you are, but you have helped everybody – and you have saved the life of Baby McMumbo.

Please come to a

THANK YOU PARTY IN YOUR HONOUR

at Bosher's sausage Shop
at 4pm this afternoon.

Everybody wants to meet you!

Yours gratefully,
The People of
Offley Street

I spent some time
in my attic
smartening up
my fur.

Quite a crowd
had gathered in
Bosher's sausage shop.

RMELIN

WITH ALL THE
GOODNESS OF SAUSAGE

KITT
CHUN

HOT DOG
FLAVOU

I felt quite nervous
but took a deep breath
and stepped forward to say
Hello.

A Mouse. But what's so bad about being a mouse?

572

mourn (mōrn) v.i. & t. Feel sorrow or regret (for or over dead person, lost thing, loss, misfortune, etc.)

mousaka or **moussaka** /mooh'sahkə/ noun a Greek dish consisting of layers of minced lamb or other meat, aubergine, tomato, and cheese with a cheese or savoury custard topping. [Modern Greek *mousakas* from Turkish *musakka*]

mouse. (*pl.* **mice**)
1a small rodent infesting houses etc.; with a pointed snout, and a long slender almost hairless tail: family Muridae. The House Mouse (Mus Musculus) has been carried around the world by Man. This **pest** causes untold damage annually to foods and materials.

heart   intestines

lungs

House mouse: mus musculus Famil
Mice may carry bacteria, viruses a
L. *mūs*, Gr. *mūs*, Skr. *mūs*;
'**steal, rob**'.

573   **mouse**

play cat and **mouse** with, torment with suspense; **mouse**~'trap, for catching mice; **mouse** ~*trap cheese*, of poor quality; timid shy person; **mou'sӯ**
2. (or -z) v.i.(Of cat, owl, etc.) hunt mice.
3. (*pl* also **mouses**) in computing, a small box, with a movable ball under it, that is connected to a computer and that, when moved across a desk or mat, causes a cursor to move across a VDU screen, so enabling the operator to point to and execute commands,
Albinos - white mice - are valuable research animals.

See also:
PESTS AND DISEASES

moustache
mousta'che, *mus-, (mustah'sh) n. Hair on either side (usu. in pl.) or both sides of (usu man's) upper lip,

MOUSTACHE. The hair on a man's upper lip when allowed to grow.

I ran
for my life,
leaving a trail
of crumbs and
cream behind me.

Back in my attic
I consulted the encyclopedia.
Unclean, Unhygienic, Unwanted.
The devastating truth was . . .

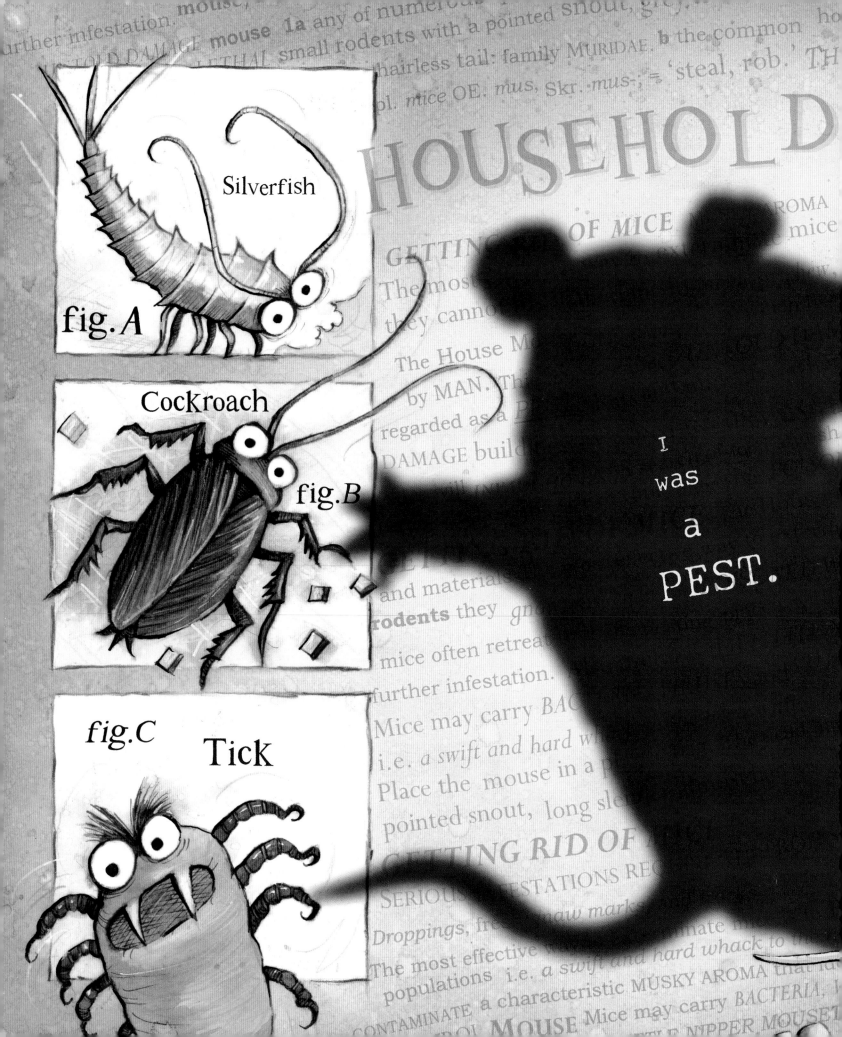

Silverfish

fig.A

Cockroach

fig.B

fig.C

Tick

I was a PEST.

Flea

fig.D

Moth

fig.E

Ant

fig.F

I felt suddenly very alone.
It was time to leave
Offley Street.

I packed up
some things
to take with me
in the morning . . .

ERMELIN

and then
sadly went to
sleep in my cheese box.

But while I was

sleeping,

someone found me.

Someone who had

followed

the trail of

crumbs and cream

that led up

the steps to

her very own attic.

And that someone

had a good look around,

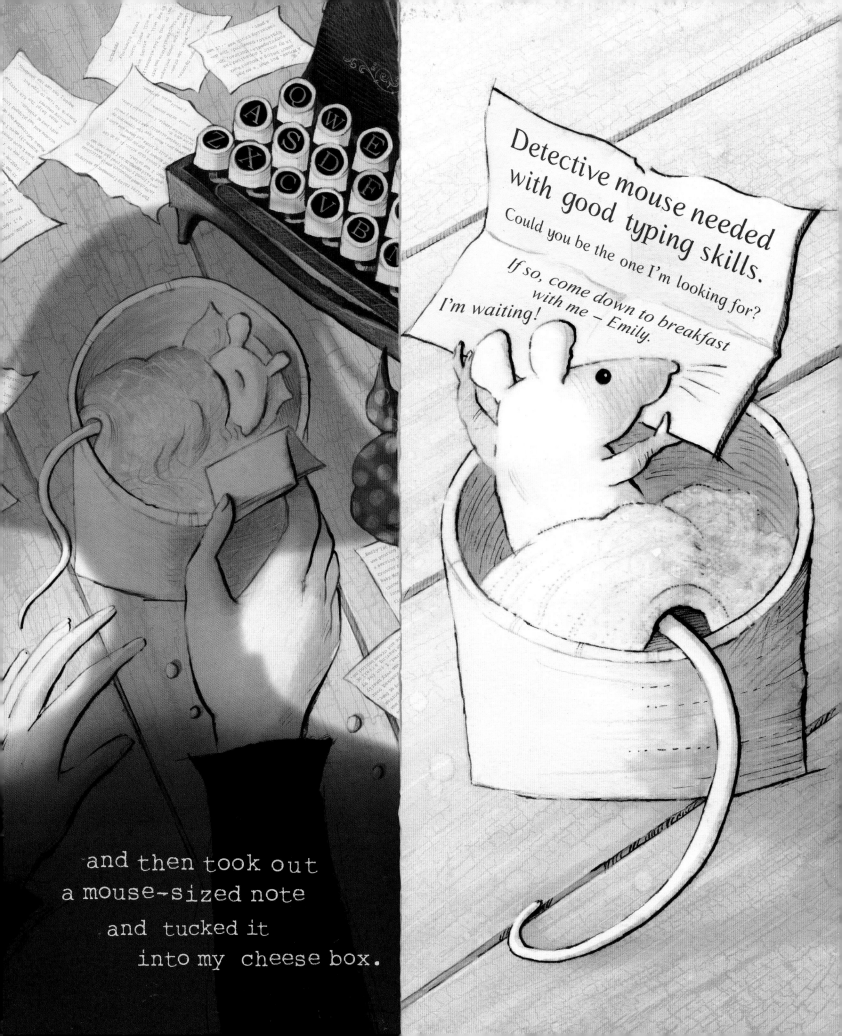

and then took out
a mouse-sized note
and tucked it
into my cheese box.

Detective mouse needed
with good typing skills.
Could you be the one I'm looking for?
If so, come down to breakfast
with me – Emily.
I'm waiting!

And now I have breakfast
every day in the kitchen
downstairs at Number 33
with Emily
(who says she is
a bit of a detective too).

We read the cereal packets
and the newspaper, and

we hunt carefully for clues,

33

because we have a plan
to start a
DETECTIVE AGENCY...

Hermelin & Emily

PRIVATE
INVESTIGATORS

You name it – we can solve it!

. . . . as Emily suspects there are
still a few mysteries to be solved
around Offley Street.